SUPERHERO STAMPEDE

By Erik Craddock

 Published in the United States by Random House Children's Books,
a division of Random House, Inc., New York. Random House and the colophon are registered trademarks of Random House, Inc.
Visit us on the Web! www.randomhouse.com/kids
Educators and librarians, for a variety of teaching tools, visit us at www.randomhouse.com/teachers
www.stonerabbit.com
Library of Congress Cataloging-in-Publication Data
Craddock, Erik.
Superhero stampede / by Erik Craddock. — 1st ed.
p. cm. — (Stone Rabbit ; 4)
Summary: After being zapped by a home-made reality transmutation device, Stone Rabbit and his friends find themselves inside the pages of their favorite comic book, waging war against a band of evildoers and trying to save the world.
ISBN 978-0-375-85877-2 (pbk.) — ISBN 978-0-375-95877-9 (lib. bdg.)
1. Graphic novels. [1. Graphic novels—Fiction. 2. Rabbits—Fiction. 3. Cartoons and comics—Fiction.
4. Superheroes—Fiction. 5. Humorous stories.] I. Title.
PZ7.7.C73Su 2010
741.5'973—dc22
2009036834
MANUFACTURED IN MALAYSIA
10 9 8 7 6 5 4 3 2 1
First Edition

Why do you always have to be such a scaredy-cat, Andy?!

Hey! I'm no scaredy-cat! I'm just a conscientious individual!
Sure you are! And I'm just vertically challenged!
Now move your wimpy butt so we can win, already! I'm not going to lose to a . . .
CRUD-MONKEYS!!!

VROOOOOOM!
YEE-HAW!

. . . girl.
Judy Goose is the winner.
Girl kicks the dumb boys' butts once again!
This game is so rigged!
Boys vs Girls R.C. Rally
SLEEPY SATURDAY SALE!
GREATEST
SLAM!

THE WORLD'S GREATEST S
Boys vs. Girls R.C. Rally
A good winner knows how to lose, young man.
Yeah, but not to some sissy girl on account of his friend being too much of a noodle-armed namby-pamby!
SLEEPY SATURDAY SALE!
ERIK CRADDOCK ENTERTAINMENT ECE
THE WORLD'S GREATEST COMICS!
HEY!
It probably comes from sitting around all day, reading comics and downing smoothies.

I think you're being a little too hard on your friend here. And graphic literature is essential to any young man's development, along with a healthy diet.
K.C.
Don't forget exercise.
Although, Andy, you could stand a little more physical activity. . . .
SALE!
SLEEPY

Fine! Go ahead and laugh! Because one of these days, I'll be tougher, stronger, faster, and meaner than all of you combined!
YOU? TOUGH? YEAH, I'D LIKE TO SEE THAT!
And I can run faster than the speed of light! Go home, Noodle Boy!
THE WORLD'S GREATEST HEROES
the Mighty Friends
25¢
JAN.

Hey, Milton! Check this out!
What's this, Judy? A salad strainer?
SLAM!
Don't be silly, Mr. Goat!
It's a Matter Algorithm Generating Initiative. But I call it Maggie for short!
Sounds dumb. What does it do?

Maggie takes whatever user-defined media is inserted into the slot here and turns it into a temporary reality. In short, it transports people right into the pages of their favorite books, allowing them to live the story.
You mean it's like a video game? SWEET!
Hey! Where do we put the quarters?

Sorry, Milton! I forgot to pay for—
SLIP!
UH-OH!
TRIP!
WWWIIIIIIIIIIIIII
THE TWISTED EVIL OF LORD MORBAD!
SHUNK!

Andy, you four-eyed klutz! Look what you've done!
SHOOM!!

STOP
BZZT!
CRACKLE!
BA - SHOOM!!!!

Behold, Planet Earth's champions of justice!
The Invisible Wrangler
Moneybags
We're the *MIGHTY FRIENDS?!*

The Jeweled Spectre
When we get back home, Andy, you're SO dead.
Captain Awesome
Speedy Dynamite

Dude! Start flying around!
And how am I supposed to do that? Controlled farting?
Spandex doesn't make the superhero, Andy! I mean, how do we even know if we have any superpowers at all?
Aw . . .
crudmonkeys!

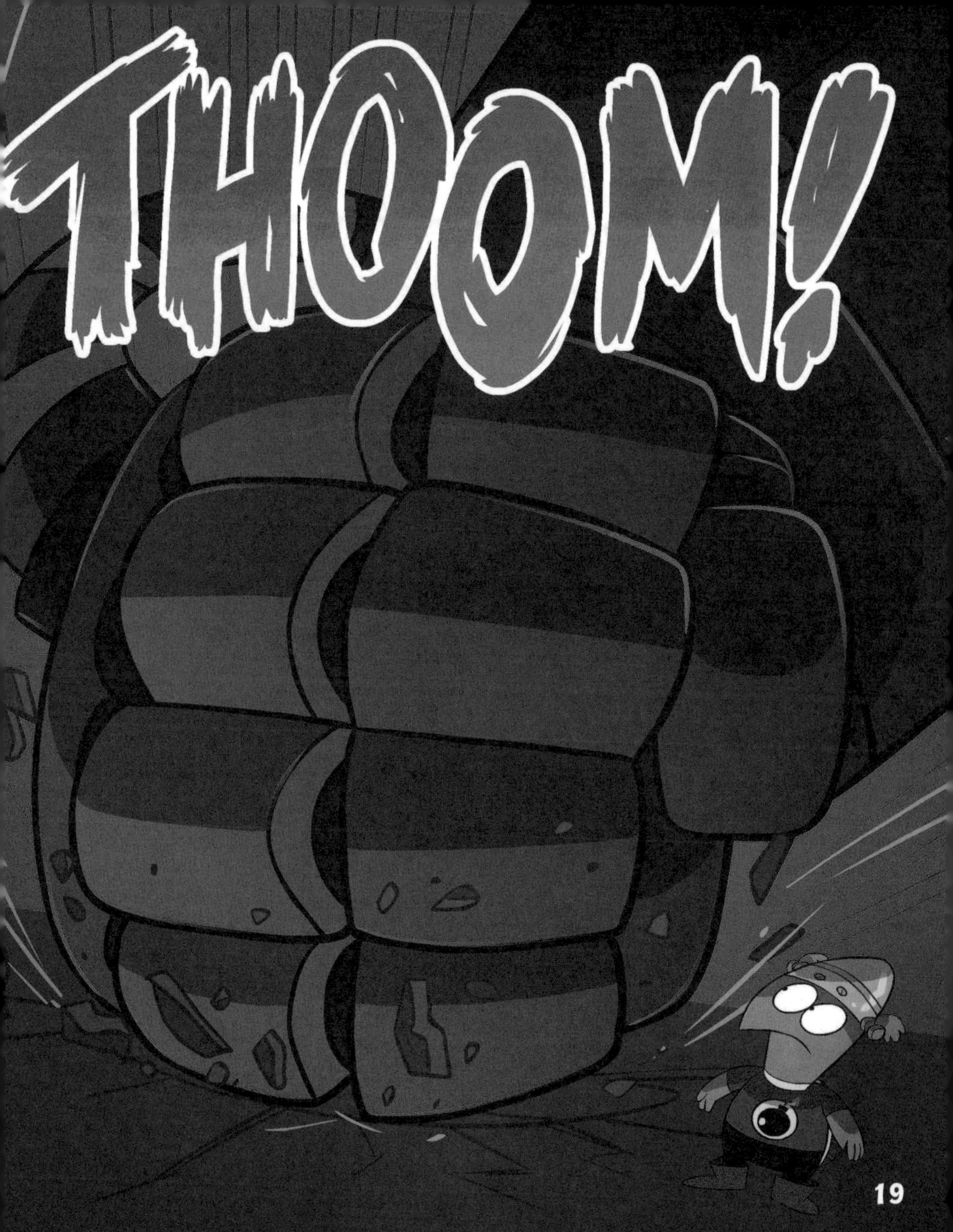

THOOM!

Well, that's one less goody two-shoes we have to concern ourselves with. . . .
Lord Morbad?

Correct, hero! It seems your powers of deduction have not yet eluded you!
Yes! I, Lord Morbad, have come to . . .

JUMPING BROCCOLI SPROUTS!
SHOVE!

Hey, Andy! You were right! We totally have superpowers!

I wonder if I have heat vision, too. Well, there's only one way to find out.

HAVE SOME OF THIS, YOU OVERGROWN CAN OF SOUP!!!

Yeah—it looks like I've got heat vision, too!

POW!

Hey! You can't do that! Especially since I have superpowers!
BA-DOOOM!
PREPARE FOR JUSTICE!!!

PITTA-PATTA-PITTA-PATTA-PITTA
PATTA-PITTA-PATTA

What the—
TiNK!
BA-DOOM!

Well, you are Speedy Dynamite.
That's my superpower? I run really, really fast and explode?
What sort of doofus writes these comics, anyway?

VOOSH!
Look out above!
OH NO!
LASSO!
Ha! Can't pummel my friends with your hand tied, can you?

Foolish hero! You think mere twine can stay my fearsome hand?
Witness the sublime fury of Concretin! The Master of Concrete!

Don't worry, kids . . .
He's gonna flatten us!
I'm too pretty to get squished!
I'll handle this.
BZZT!

The Jeweled Spectre, using the power of his mystic gauntlets, travels through the shadow realm to ambush the evil Concretin. . . .
There's that little megalomaniac.

Young man! You need to stop causing trouble this instant!
VOOSH!
Oh really? And what, pray tell, do you plan to do if I refuse, you *old goat*?!

JIM DANDY
SLUGGER™

SHOOM!
This.

THWAK!
I think I might have hit the bleachers on that one.
AAAAAAAAA!

You may have bested Concretin—but now you face *The Iceberg!*
What's his superpower? Bad taste in hats? Teach this guy a lesson, Andy!
But I have no superpowers! All I am is a billionaire playboy!
POOM!

NOW you tell me!

The package is ready for extraction!
Excellent. We leave at once!

Farewell, heroes! When next we meet, it shall be . . .
. . . your DOOM!
Hey! They're taking Andy!

HA! HA! HA! HA! HAAA!
ANDY! WHERE'S ANDY?!
Poof!

Several hours later . . .
What . . .
where . . .
The Dastardly Trifecta!
Indeed, Moneybags! Quite astute! Welcome . . .

. . . to the FORTRESS OF EVIL!!!

Torture me! Beat me up and take my lunch money! But I would never sell out my friends! No way, no—
Would you like some cake?

Cake?
But of course, what else would it be? We baked it just for you, after all. . . .

Is it poison?
No, actually it's vanilla butter pecan.
And it even comes with robotic legs! Try some!
SHUNK!
SHUNK!
Well, okay . . . but if it's poison I'm gonna get mad . . . and you wouldn't like me when I'm mad!
SCOOP!

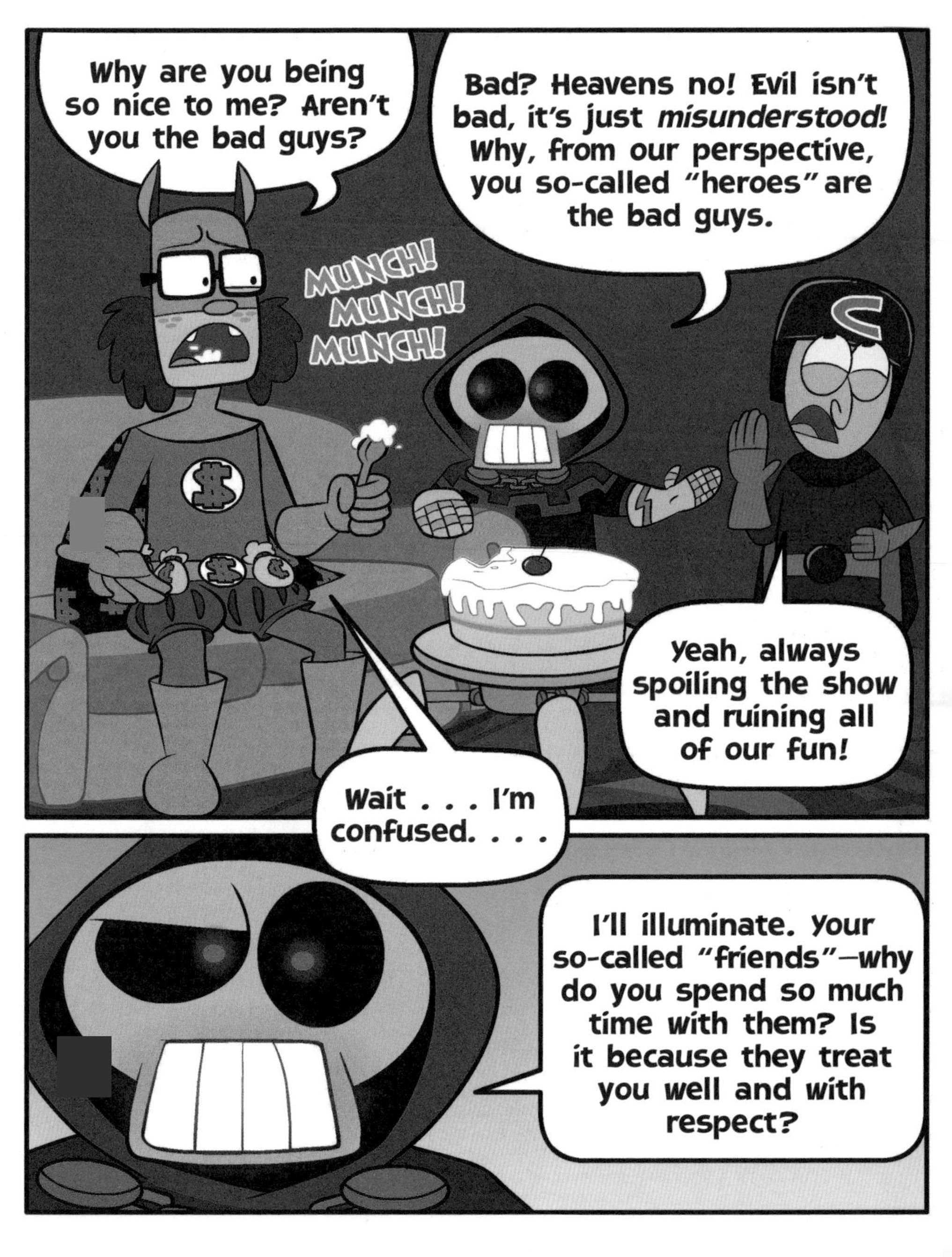
Why are you being so nice to me? Aren't you the bad guys?
Bad? Heavens no! Evil isn't bad, it's just *misunderstood*! Why, from our perspective, you so-called "heroes" are the bad guys.
MUNCH! MUNCH! MUNCH!
Yeah, always spoiling the show and ruining all of our fun!
Wait . . . I'm confused. . . .
I'll illuminate. Your so-called "friends"—why do you spend so much time with them? Is it because they treat you well and with respect?

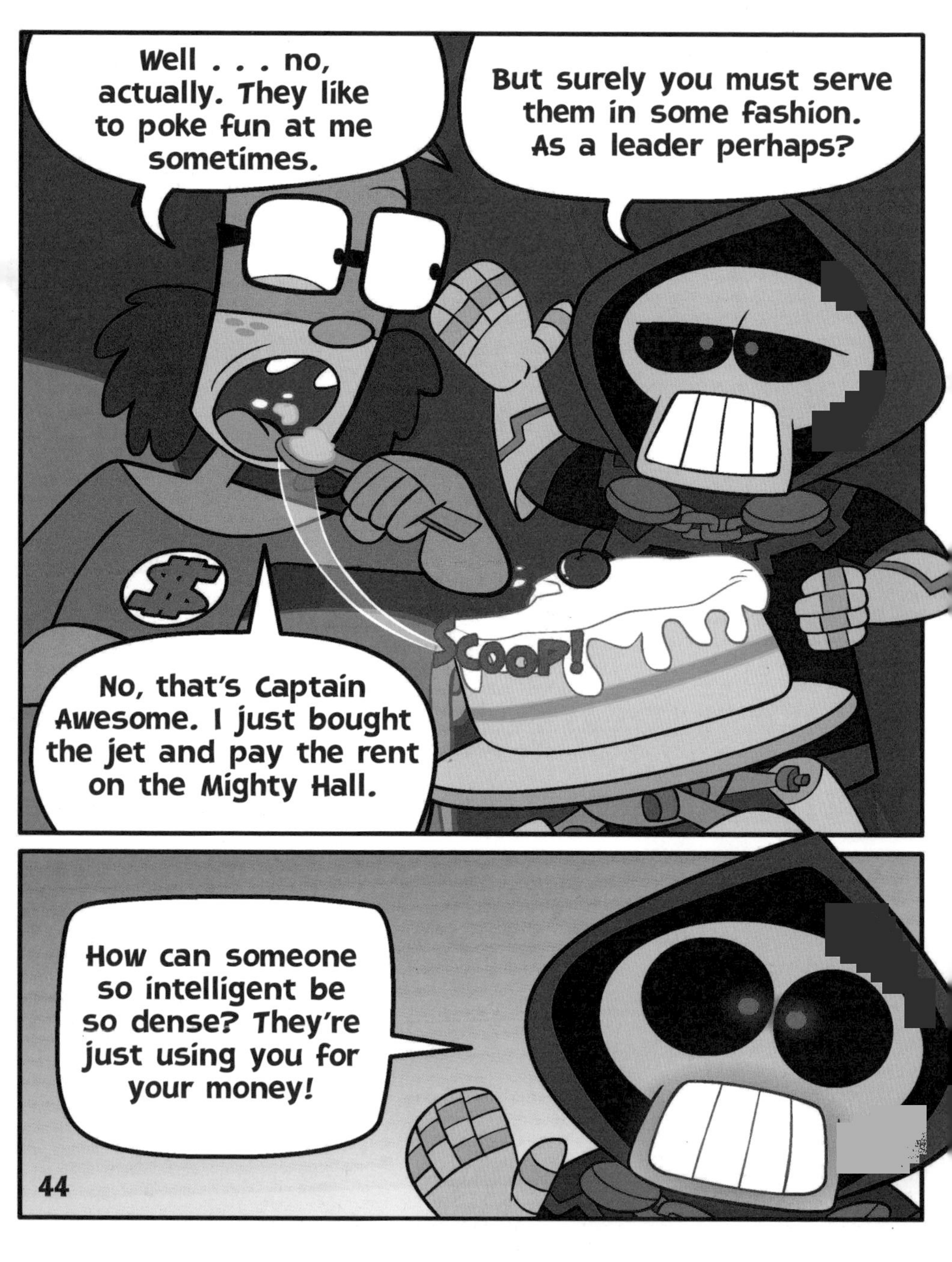
Well . . . no, actually. They like to poke fun at me sometimes.
But surely you must serve them in some fashion. As a leader perhaps?
SCOOP!
No, that's Captain Awesome. I just bought the jet and pay the rent on the Mighty Hall.
How can someone so intelligent be so dense? They're just using you for your money!

That's a lie, and you know it!

Is that so? When was the last time they complimented you? Or baked you a cake? Or told you how much they appreciate your contribution to the team?

You're . . . you're a liar! A big fat liar!
If I'm lying, then why are you crying? Your tears only serve to prove my hypothesis.

They're not your friends, Andy. They never were. And now we must make them pay for humiliating you all those years!

NOOOOOO!
SMACK!
They're my friends!! My . . . friends. . . .
Fear not. . . . We're your friends now.

Meanwhile, in the Mighty Hall . . .
Smooth move, Dumb Ears! Faster than a speeding bullet, my eye!
Oh! And you should talk, Shell for Brains! Why didn't you just vibrate your legs at hyperspeed in order to melt the ice? Ever think of that?
No! Because I don't waste my time reading stupid comic books like you do, Captain Loser!
Boys! Boys! Calm down!

Can't you turn this thing off? Can't you just make things go back to normal?
I can't! Once the events are set in motion, we have to wait until the event cycle decays.
Can anyone tell me what Spunky Einstein here just said?!
She said we have to wait until the story in the comic ends. And your panicking doesn't exactly help matters, either, young man!
Yeah, Dumb Ears!

I just don't want to see my best friend ripped to smithereens by a group of supervillains. I mean, where do we even begin looking for Andy?
CRASH!
BRRRRKTZ!

CANDY CANE LANE TONIGHT
Well, that works.

Meanwhile, at the Fortress of Evil . . .
We greatly appreciate your willingness to disclose the Mighty Friends' secret weaknesses to us. Total victory is now assured!

As for your suit, it is infused with megalomite— space crystals that sap Captain Awesome's superpowers.
It wasn't easy harvesting this mineral, seeing how it was on the other side of the universe. But it will all be worth it when you annihilate those "mighty" friends. . . .

Wow . . . this place totally needs a new name.
All right, kids. Let's find Andy. Stick together and keep an eye out.
Welcome to Candy Cane Lane
the WORST place ever!

Who knows what we're going to be up against in this place.

Have a nice slice of your only weakness, Speedy!
Oh no! Boysenberry!
WITH LOVE
WAP!

Henri?
Keep your eyes open, kids. We don't want to get—
Hey! Where'd Henri go?

Ack! My powers!
SCHLOMP!

Hey, come back here with Milton, you criminal!
No, wait! Stop!
Don't go! It's a trap!

OH NO! *MILTON!* Hang on, I'm—
This appleberry perfume should stop you in your tracks!

POOF!
PARFUM

Great! Just great! Now everybody's gone! How can things possibly get any worse?!
THOOM!!

AW, CRUDMONKEYS!

THWAK!
OOK!
ACK!
POOM!
EEK!
BIFF!
BONK!

STOMP!
STOMP!
STOMP!
STOMP!
Wow! That punch actually hurt!
BOOM!

Andy . . .
is that you?

CRUNCH!
AUGH! MY EARS! LET GO OF MY EARS!
Andy, what are you doing?
TOSS!

BAKOOM!

Hey! What gives, buddy? We were looking all over for you. And now you're–

POW!
Paying you back for years of name-calling!

For years of pushing me around!
BOOM!

And for years of pretending to be my friend!
SLAM!
CRUNCH!

But I have REAL friends now!
People who can truly appreciate me for who I am!
SNAP!
Wait! You've got to listen to me, Andy! I don't know what those guys were telling you, but—
Andy? I'm no longer "Andy"!

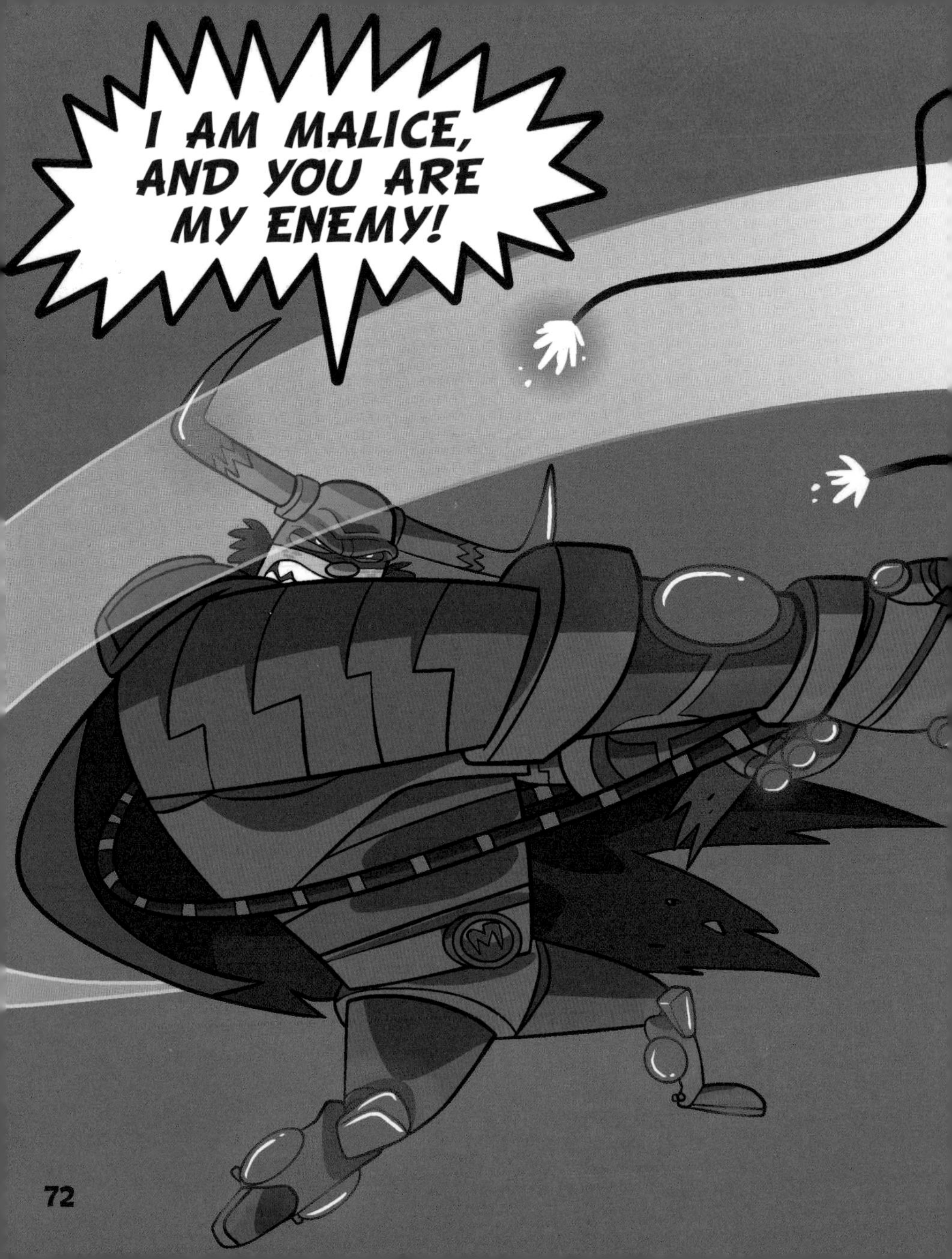
I AM MALICE, AND YOU ARE MY ENEMY!

POW!

BASH!
SLAM!
OUCH

THOOM!
CLAP!

Well played, Malice! Bravo!
Andy, is that you?! What have you done?
Why would you do such a thing?
I—I thought we were pals?! Chums!

Silence! You mean nothing to me! You're nothing more than hypocrites and liars!
You all called me a scaredy-cat! You said I was a noodle-armed namby-pamby! You even said I had four eyes! Friends don't do that.
Andy, I don't know what those sick little men put in your head. But we're your friends! Not THEM! Don't listen to their lies!

Yeah, but we were just messing around! I don't exactly have washboard abs. And Dumb Ears can't even lift five pounds!
And Milton and I both wear glasses, too!

Andy . . . we did go too far at the comic shop. We were wrong to make fun of you then.

But those creeps over there aren't your friends—we are. The second you stop being useful to them, they'll get rid of you faster than yesterday's gym socks.
And no real friend would ever throw another friend away.
Besides, who else am I going to watch the *Ultradude* show with? Not Dumb Ears, that's for sure!

I-I don't know what to do!!!

BEEP! BEEP! BEEP!
Luckily, we do!
CLICK!

I'm afraid that we've had a contingency plan for this situation, you ungrateful wretch!
Word of advice: never take the cake!

YOU LEAVE ANDY ALONE!
KOOM!
Andy! Are you okay?
I'm—really sorry about all of this.

It's okay, buddy. Can you walk?
I think so, but the suit's all busted.
Where do you two think you are going? We haven't finished having our fun yet.
SWOOP!
SWOOP!
CLAP!

CRUNCH!
CRUNCH!
CRUNCH!
Heh! He didn't see that one coming!
All too easy . . .

Hey, w-wait a minute! Something's wrong—
RUMBLE! RUMBLE! RUMBLE!
ARGH! HE BROKE MY LITTLE MITTENS!
KER-

SHAPOW!

It looks like all those years spent reading comics are finally paying off—I love being solar-powered!

Time to finish this!
Clearly your long-eared friend has chosen to abandon you. Now face the unbridled fury of—
Look! Up in the sky! It's a bird!
It's a plane!
No, it's *Dumb Ears!* And he's coming *STRAIGHT AT US!*

THOOM!

Hey, guys! What do supervillains get for lunch from the Mighty Hall cafeteria?
W-we don't know! What do they g-get?
SHIVER! SHIVER! SHIVER!
Give up?
SHIVER! SHIVER!
A knuckle sandwich!

POW!
KER-
POW!

Clever joke. But you won't find being disintegrated into a quadrillion atoms quite as amusing! Farewell, do-gooder!
CLICK!
What?! NO!
BLING!

No! This cannot be!
SSSCCHHH-
POW!
And that's what buddies are for. . . .
Thanks, Andy.
SIZZLE.
SIZZLE.

Event cycle complete!
Now reverting to singular reality!
Hmph! It's about time.

Well, I'm glad that's over with!
Hey! I thought it was kind of fun.
I especially liked the part where Andy threw Dumb Ears around like a rag doll.
SALE!

Judy, I don't mean to stifle your creativity, but next time please consider the consequences of your actions before you decide to alter the space-time continuum.
So what are you going to do now?
Oh no, Mr. Goat, I'm through with quantum physics. If you ask me, it gets kind of boring after a while.
ERIK CRADDOCK ENTERTAINMENT
ECE
THE WORLD'S GREATEST COMICS!

Simple. I'm going to create hyperintelligent robotic teddy bears that can do all of the boring stuff for me!
Somehow, I know this won't end well. . . .
RTB - 001
BOYS VS. GIRLS
THE END.